SSSSNAP! MISTER SHARK

About the author

Neal Zetter is a London-based comedy performance poet, author and entertainer with a huge following in schools. He has been using poetry writing and performance to develop literacy, confidence, self-expression and creativity in 3 to 103 year olds for over twenty years and his book **Bees in My Bananas** won the 2015 Wishing Shelf Independent Book Award. As well as schools, Neal has performed at comedy and poetry clubs, theatres, pubs, music venues, and the Royal Festival Hall. He lives in east London.

His most recent poetry collection available from Troika Books is **It's Not Fine to Sit on a Porcupine**.

See **www.cccpworkshops.co.uk** for information about Neal's work.

About the illustrator

Chris White is an illustrator, writer and poet. He has created several popular characters including *Bitey the Veggie Vampire* and illustrated many people's work including Neal Zetter's **Bees in My Bananas**. Chris has featured on radio and TV and travelled around the world bringing his cartoon and rhyme roadshows alive for lots of people.

For Troika he has illustrated **ODD SOCKS!** and **SSSSNAP! MISTER SHARK**.

See **www.veggievampire.com** for information about Chris's work.

Published by TROIKA BOOKS

First published 2016

Troika Books
Well House, Green Lane, Ardleigh CO7 7PD
www.troikabooks.com

A CIP catalogue record for this book is available from the British Library

ISBN 978-1-909991-35-4

1 2 3 4 5 6 7 8 9 10

Printed in Poland

SSSSNAP! MISTER SHARK

Neal Zetter

Illustrated by

Chris White

troika books

Mister Shark, don't bite my hand!

Mister Shark, don't bite my toes!

Mister Shark, don't bite my ear!

Mister Shark, don't bite my nose!

Mister Shark, don't bite my chest!

Mister Shark, don't bite my cheek!

Mister Shark, don't bite my hair!

Mister Shark, don't bite my feet!

Mister Shark, don't bite my knee!

Mister Shark, don't bite my thumb!

Mister Shark, don't bite my back!

Mister Shark, don't bite my bum!

Mister Shark, don't eat me up!

PLEASE

Mister Shark, keep your jaws shut!